SCORE FOR IMAGINATION
A *Lola Jones* BOOK

JONATHAN EIG

illustrated by
ALICIA TEBA GODOY

ALBERT WHITMAN & CO.
Chicago, Illinois

For Lillian, Jeffery, and Lola—JE

To my friend and sister, Alba—ATG

ﳙﳙﳙ

Library of Congress Cataloging-in-Publication data
is on file with the publisher.

Text copyright © 2020 by Jonathan Eig
Illustrations copyright © 2020 by Albert Whitman & Company
Illustrations by Alicia Teba Godoy
First published in the United States of America
in 2020 by Albert Whitman & Company
ISBN 978-0-8075-6565-0 (hardcover)
ISBN 978-0-8075-6569-8 (paperback)
ISBN 978-0-8075-6567-4 (ebook)

Printed in the United States of America
10 9 8 7 6 5 4 3 2 1 LB 24 23 22 21 20

Design by Aphelandra Messer

For more information about Albert Whitman & Company,
visit our website at www.albertwhitman.com.

TABLE OF CONTENTS

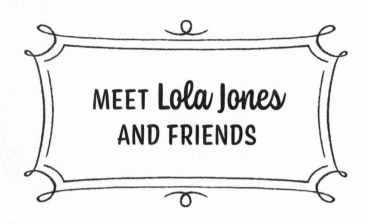

MEET Lola Jones AND FRIENDS

Hi! I'm Lola.
I love books and
I love adventure.
When I'm trying to
solve a problem, I
know I can count on
my family, my friends,
and characters from my
favorite books!

Lola Jones

Lillian Jones
I'm Lola's mother.
I love playing soccer
and having crazy
dance parties with
my daughter.

Grampa Ed
I'm Lola's grandfather.
That kid cracks me up.
I try to pretend I'm
grumpy sometimes,
but she never
falls for it.

Mrs. Gunderson
I'm Lola's teacher,
and I love my third
graders. My favorite
book is *Charlotte's
Web* by E.B. White.

Maya and **Fayth**
We're Lola's best friends.
Whatever wild plan she's hatching,
we're always there to help out!

1.
Pancakes and Practice

It was broad daylight when Lola got up, rubbed her eyes, and looked out her bedroom window. Sunshine brightened the brick wall of the building next door. A feathery cloud floated above the building. Above that, an airplane made a white chalk line across the rectangle of blue sky.

For a moment, Lola thought she had overslept and missed school. She sat up in bed as a feeling of dread clutched her stomach like a cold metal claw.

And then the claw let go. Today was Saturday! No school!

On Saturday, Grampa Ed made chocolate-chip pancakes! On Saturday, her mother would take her to the park to practice soccer! And who knows what else might happen? Absolutely anything! On a sunshiny Saturday in the city there was lots of scope for imagination. That's what Anne in *Anne of Green Gables* would say. Lola was on page 132. It was her latest favorite book.

Lola bounced out of bed, pulled on a pair of shorts and a T-shirt, and went to the kitchen. Grampa Ed stood at the counter, cracking eggs.

"Morning, kid," said Grampa Ed.

"Good morning, Grampa." Lola gave her grandpa big hug.

"How many pancakes do you want?" he asked.

"Seventy-seven," Lola said. "Wait, make it seventy-eight. I'm starving."

Grampa wrinkled his bushy eyebrows. "How about three?"

"Good enough! Thanks, Grampa."

Lola Jones was eight and a half. She was small

for her age but a strong and fast runner, which was good for soccer. She had dark hair and eyes and a voice that squeaked when she got excited.

From the kitchen, she could see out the window and down to the alley, which was long and narrow and dotted with plastic garbage bins in three different colors: black, green, and blue. At the east end of the alley was a big street with rushing cars and buses; at the west end was a

smaller street with parked cars and slower-moving traffic. At both ends there were handsome brick buildings and towering elm trees and oak trees. The trees, Lola thought, looked like they were trying on new green leaves for spring. Lola went to the back door and opened it to check the weather.

"Isn't this the loveliest day, Grampa?" she asked. "I don't think I could even imagine a lovelier day than this one. Could you?"

"Yeah, I suppose the alley is beautiful if you like garbage trucks." Grampa Ed gave a little laugh. "What's gotten into you? Did you take extra-happy pills this morning?"

Lola paused, surprised.

"Oh, Grampa, is there *really* such a thing as happy pills? I suppose you're teasing. But if there is, I think that would be a *wonderful* invention, even though I wouldn't need them today, because I'm already super happy. Because it's Saturday, Grampa! And you're making pancakes! And Mom's going to take me to the park to practice soccer! And Anne of Green Gables sees beauty everywhere she looks. 'Scope for imagination,' she calls it. And I guess she's got me thinking that way too. There's so much scope for imagination on a day like today in a wonderful city like ours! Even the alley is beautiful when the sun is up and the streetlights are still on and the puddles reflect their shimmering light!"

"Eat your pancakes, kid. If I have to listen to any more of this cheerfulness my head's going to explode. I haven't even had my coffee yet, for crying out loud."

"Oh, I'll make your coffee, Grampa!" Lola loved making coffee. Grampa Ed taught her how when she was little and now she was an expert.

As Lola went to the cabinet to take out Grampa's coffee cup, her mother came into the kitchen. Lillian Jones was already dressed for soccer in green sweatpants and a gray sweatshirt, with her brown hair tied in two short pigtails.

"Good morning, sweetie," she said, hugging Lola first, then leaning in to peck Grampa Ed on his stubbly cheek.

"Hey, Lillian..." Grampa Ed's voice was deep and scratchy. He had hairy arms and a bunch of tattoos, including one on his arm that read *Whatever Lola Wants.* "Isn't it the most beautiful morning ever? The garbage trucks smell like flowers and it's super-duper great to be alive!"

He smiled and gave Lola a wink. She cracked up.

Lillian Jones scrunched her eyebrows and looked at her daughter, hoping she would explain Grampa Ed's behavior.

"I think he took too many happy pills!" Lola giggled. "Either that or he's been reading *Anne of Green Gables*!"

"I need to start getting up earlier," Lola's mother said. "I can never understand what's going on when I walk in on you guys. Anyway, finish your pancakes and let's go, girl. We've got work to do on the soccer field!"

2.
The Recess Match

A boy named Gabriel Contento lived at the east end of Lola's block, in a third-floor apartment. Gabriel's window faced the alley. When he played games and watched videos on his computer, he kept a sharp eye on the alley, from one end to the other, so that he knew when a kid got a new bike or skateboard or when a grown-up got a new car. If you walked your dog and didn't pick up the dog's poop, or picked it up and dropped it in one of the blue

or green recycling bins where it didn't belong, Gabriel probably knew about it.

When he saw Lola and her mother walking down the alley, Lola gently kicking a soccer ball, he thought about shouting "hello" out the window to her, or at least just waving. But he didn't. They were in the same grade,

but not the same class. Some kids made friends easily. Gabriel wasn't one of them.

Lola and her mother walked to the park.

"Don't take it easy on me today, Mom," Lola said.

"I won't."

"I mean it! I have to get better."

"You're taking these soccer games seriously," Lola's mom said.

"You would too if you were playing," Lola said. "It's a battle for the ages. It's *epochal*. That's a new word I learned. I'm trying to get more big words. Anne of Green Gables says you have to have big words if you want to express big ideas. Anyway, *epochal* means marking a big event or a big period in life."

"What's so *epochal* about these soccer games?" Lola's mom asked.

"Well, you know our playground, right? It's small. So, there's only room for one soccer game at a time at recess. And if the first graders get there before us third graders, we can't play at all.

If the third-grade *boys* get there first, they don't let the girls play. And if Mr. Nick tells them they *have* to let all the kids play, the boys don't pass to us and they don't let us take throw-ins or penalty kicks. It's a real *predicament*. That's another big word I learned. It means 'mess.'"

"That sure is a *predicament*," her mother said.

They got to the park and Lola took off, running across the grass as fast as she could.

"Kick the ball so I have to run for it!" Lola shouted, and her mother did.

They played for hours. When Lola finally got tired, she and her mother took the bus to the library, where Lola asked the librarian to recommend a book about soccer strategy.

"Let me show you my favorite," the librarian said. She pulled out a book called *Smarter Soccer*. "It doesn't have any pictures, but I think you'll like it."

With her soccer ball under one arm and her new book under the other, Lola walked out of the library. She and her mother took the bus home.

ee

The following Monday, when the bell rang for recess, Lola and three other girls hurried to the playground to claim the soccer field before the boys got there. They were too late. As usual, Gabriel Contento was sitting on a soccer ball in front of one of the two goals. Though he never played, Gabriel, somehow, almost always got to the field before anyone else, reserving the ball and the field for the third-grade boys.

"Hey, Gabriel!" Lola yelled. "How about letting us use that ball until the boys get here?"

"Sorry," Gabriel said.

"Then how about this? Let's be on the same team!" Lola raised both hands. "Pass me the ball and I'll pass it back to you."

"No thanks," he said. "I'm the coach."

A bunch of boys burst through the double doors and ran across the playground. Gabriel gently kicked the ball to Tommy Adkins.

The playground was small and had three parts: the jungle gym, with its slides and monkey bars; the basketball court, with its lone backboard and hoop atop a metal pole; and the soccer field, where the cracked blacktop was painted green with white lines to resemble a grassy field.

As the boys began passing the soccer ball across the blacktop, Lola and the girls spread out across the field.

"We're playing, too!" Lola shouted.

"Sorry," Tommy Adkins shouted back. "The game already started."

"Did not!" answered Fayth.

Mr. Nick stepped across the field and put his foot on the ball. Mr. Nick was a giant. Everyone said he used to be a champion boxer but quit boxing because it was too easy and he got tired of knocking people out.

"Pick teams and get started," he said as he kicked the ball to Lola. "Everyone plays."

Recess lasted only twenty minutes, so they had no time to waste. Tommy Adkins and Howie

Allen—the two best boy athletes in third grade—volunteered to be captains. They quickly picked teams, four boys and three girls on each side. Lola was the last one picked. She was on Howie's team.

"Howieeeeee! Howieeeeee! I'm open!" she shouted as she raced around. She really was open, sometimes, but Howie never passed the ball to her. None of the boys did.

Fayth and Maya tried, too. "Howieeeeee! Howieeeeee!"

The boys never passed the ball to the girls, never congratulated them when they made a good play, and never looked them in the eyes.

When the bell rang, the game ended. Lola's team lost, six goals to four.

"That was so unfair," Lola said, wiping her sweaty forehead and tucking her hair behind her ears.

"So, so, *sooo* unfair!" Fayth said.

"They pretend they don't see us!" Lola said.

"Like we're invisible!" agreed Maya.

"Did you see how Tommy stole the ball from Sevilla?" Fayth said. "And they were on the same team!"

"They don't even care about winning," Lola said. "All they want to do is score goals."

"And make sure we *don't*!" said Maya.

"I'm so mad!" Lola said.

"My brother says don't get mad...get even!" Maya said.

"That's a good idea," Lola said. "Maybe if we get more girls tomorrow, the teams will be more even and we can make it harder for them to ignore us."

"Yeah," Fayth said. "Mr. Nick says everybody plays. No subs. So if we get ten girls, we can take over the game."

"That'll be *epochal*!" Lola said.

Maya and Fayth, who knew all about Lola's new interest in big words, waited for the definition.

"That means it'll be a game-changer!" Lola said.

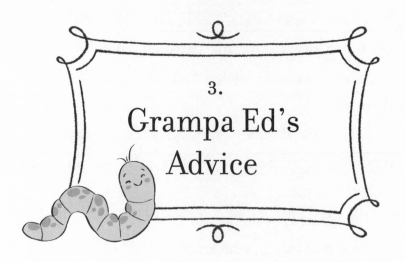

3.
Grampa Ed's Advice

When Lola got home from school on Monday, her mother was still at work. Lillian Jones worked for the police department and that meant she never knew exactly when she would get home because crime didn't happen on a schedule. Lola went downstairs to visit Grampa Ed, who lived in the first-floor apartment and also had an art studio there. It was messy, but Lola loved it.

"Hey, kid, how was school?" Grampa Ed looked up from his art table as Lola came in the door. He had a pencil in one hand and a big pink eraser in the other.

Lola took a deep breath. Grampa's apartment smelled warm and sweet and sour all at the same time. She moved carefully to make sure she didn't step on a pencil, a plastic cup, or a paint brush. "We lost, six to four," she said. "The girls didn't even get to touch the ball."

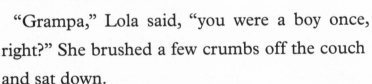

"I asked about school, not recess," Grampa Ed said. "Did you learn anything?"

"I learned boys don't play well with girls."

"That's an important lesson, I guess." Grampa Ed scratched his bald head with his eraser.

"Grampa," Lola said, "you were a boy once, right?" She brushed a few crumbs off the couch and sat down.

"Sure was."

"Did you do a lot of boy stuff?"

"Like what?"

"Like burping and cutting the heads off dolls and digging up earthworms and putting them in the teacher's lunch and hogging the soccer ball?"

"Have you been reading my old report cards?" Grampa laughed.

"I'm serious. Did you do stuff like that, Grampa?"

"Burping and earthworms, yes. Cutting heads off dolls, no. Why?"

"Well, I was just thinking that maybe if I tried to understand the boys, I could convince them to play fair. I could appeal to their sense of *camaraderie*. That means mutual friendship and trust."

"Oh yeah, I know that word," Grampa said. "But I hate to tell you, I think you're wasting your time."

"Why?"

"Well, when I was a boy I was a lot more concerned with winning than playing fair. If you want to convince the boys to play fair, you're going to have to do more than ask them. You're going to have to prove to them that your way is better. And you probably have to prove it a few times before they get it. We're a stubborn bunch."

"Grampa! That's terrible! I can't believe you're saying that boys won't respond to a call for *camaraderie*."

"Well, I guess we'll see," Grampa said. "In the meantime, it wouldn't hurt to keep practicing."

Lola rubbed her chin.

"Grampa," she said, "can I tell you a secret?"

Grampa put down his pencil and eraser, put his hands on his lap, and waited for Lola to speak.

"Well...," she said. "It's a little embarrassing."

"I don't know if you've noticed, kid," Grampa said, "but I'm sort of crazy about you. I don't think there's anything you can say that's going to change that."

"OK." Lola took a deep breath. "Well..." She lowered her voice until the sound hardly came out at all. "I'm...um...pretty... um...bad at soccer."

Grampa waited. And then he rolled his eyes and laughed. "Is that *it*?"

"You shouldn't laugh," she said. "It's embarrassing! It's like my feet get nervous around the ball. They never do what I want them to do. No matter how much I practice, I don't get better!"

"So, quit," Grampa said. "Switch to ping-pong. Or chess."

"No way, Grampa! I'm not quitting soccer. I love soccer! And you don't have to be good at something to love it. That's what Anne of Green Gables says. She says that after trying and winning, trying and failing is the next best thing, because the trying is exactly the same in both cases. Trying is the important part."

"OK, then don't quit." Grampa picked up his pencil. "Keep trying. Hey, maybe you can ask that kid Gabriel from down the street to give you some pointers. I hear he's good."

"Wait…You know Gabriel?"

"I know his grandfather, Francisco. He says his kids and his grandkids are all soccer stars. Maybe you and Gabriel could practice after school."

Lola sank deep into thought. If Gabriel was good at soccer, why didn't he play? Maybe he was hiding something from his grandfather, or maybe there was something about Gabriel that Lola hadn't figured out.

"Well, what do you say?" Grampa asked. "Why don't you ring the kid's doorbell and ask him to practice?"

"I don't know," Lola said. "It's complicated."

"Why, because he's a boy? Are you afraid he's going to dig up earthworms and put them in your lunch?"

"No." Lola laughed. "But I'm pretty sure he won't want to help a girl."

Lola got off the couch and went upstairs to her room. She flopped down on the bed and stared up at her poster of Team USA. All

the women on the team were so big and strong. But they must have been eight and a half years old once, too. They must have played with boys like Tommy Adkins and Howie Allen who never passed the ball to girls. What did *they* do about it?

As her eyes moved across the picture, from one player to the next, Lola made up her mind. She was definitely *not* going to ring Gabriel's doorbell to ask for help.

The third-grade boys were the problem, not the solution!

4.
Cavemen

At recess the next day, Lola and her friends were ready. This time they brought twelve girls. When the captains got done picking teams, there were six girls and four boys on each team.

"This is going to be awesome," Lola said. "We're going to *vanquish* them."

"Wait! I know that one," Fayth said. "It means defeat, right?"

"Yes!" Lola smiled and pumped her fist.

Before the game began, Gabriel huddled with Tommy and Howie. Lola thought that was strange because Howie and Tommy were on opposing teams. How could Gabriel coach both sides?

Lola walked over to the huddle. "Excuse me, but what are you talking about?"

"We're talking about strategy," Gabriel said. He held the soccer ball under one arm.

"I want to talk about the strategy, too," Lola said. "Howie and I are on the same team."

Gabriel shrugged. "Sorry."

"That's not nice," Lola said, as she tugged the ball from Gabriel's arm and tossed it to Fayth. "You're wasting time. Let's play!"

They played. But having extra girls on the field didn't help. The boys worked harder than ever to keep the ball away from girls. At the start of the game, Fayth made a perfect pass to Lola at midfield. Fayth cut toward the goal and shouted for Lola to pass it back, but before Lola could make the pass, Howie gave Lola a bump and stole the ball.

"Howie! We're on the same team!" Lola shouted.

But Howie was already gone.

The game ended in a tie, two to two.

The rest of the day in school Lola struggled to pay attention. She was too angry. Her teacher,

Mrs. Gunderson, asked her if she was feeling sick. Lola said she was fine. But she was still upset later that afternoon as she walked home from school with Maya and Fayth.

"It's like they don't even want to win if we're helping them do it!" Maya said.

"I think they *do* want to win, sort of," Fayth said. "But it's more important for them to prove that boys are better than girls. They're behaving like a bunch of kindergartners."

"Kindergarten *boys*, you mean," Lola added. "Kindergarten *girls* would never do that stuff."

"I don't understand it," said Maya.

"I do," said Fayth. "That's how my brothers behave all the time. My mother calls them cave-men. She says they haven't evolved."

"Do you think cavemen ever let cavewomen play soccer?"

"Probably not," said Maya. "The cavewomen probably had to stay home and knit the soccer balls out of deerskin or something."

"Well, that's history," Lola said. "Ancient history."

When she got home, Lola gave Grampa Ed another report.

"The score was two to two," she said.

"A tie isn't so bad," Grampa said.

"It's not the score that made me mad. It's the way the boys played." Lola frowned. "Grampa, do you think boys act like cavemen?"

"I guess so…sometimes," Grampa Ed said. "But, hey, cavemen can learn. Some smart caveman figured out how to make fire. Another one invented the cell phone."

Lola had the feeling Grampa Ed was joking about the cell phone, just like the happy pills, but she let it go.

"But, Grampa, how do you know it wasn't a cavewoman who invented fire? You don't know at all!"

Grampa Ed rubbed his bald head.

"That's the thing," Lola said. "You boys

have all this extra confidence. Too much! You think you invented *everything*. You think you should get the ball on the soccer field and the girls should get out of the way. You think if you keep treating us badly, we'll give up. But we don't have to give up. We're not going to!"

"You're right," Grampa Ed said. "Sorry. I should not have assumed that a caveman invented fire. But, hey, maybe I can help."

"How?"

"Well, your mother showed me that soccer book you borrowed from the library." Grampa Ed picked up *Smarter Soccer* from his drawing table. "Your mother thought the book would be easier to understand if it had pictures. So I read a few chapters and made illustrations. Here, let me show you."

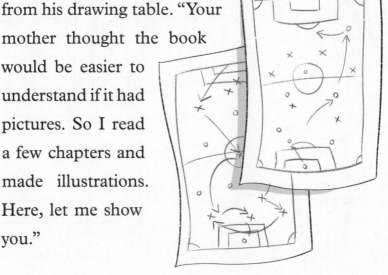

Lola flipped through Grampa Ed's drawings.

"Wow, these are beautiful." She rubbed her chin. "But wait, there's something wrong. There's no ball in these pictures. If there were a ball, wouldn't all the players be near the ball?"

"I don't know," Grampa Ed said, "because I didn't understand all the soccer terms in the book. But I think the author is saying you don't have to run around as much if you know what you're doing."

"Interesting," Lola said.

"Oh, and there's one more thing," Grampa Ed said. "I invited Gabriel and his grandfather over for dinner Friday."

Lola dropped the drawings and stood up.

"You did *what?*" Her voice squeaked.

Grampa Ed shrugged.

"But, Grampa, I told you, Gabriel is part of the problem. He's one of the cavemen!"

"Well, you know what they say..."

Lola interrupted. "Grampa, I *really* don't want Gabriel coming over here for dinner."

Grampa Ed pretended he wasn't listening.

"You know what they say," he continued. "Keep your friends close...and keep your enemies closer."

Lola shook her head, frustrated.

"Grampa," she said, "I love you, but trust me... no kid would *ever* listen to that advice."

5.
The Stuck Clock

The classroom clock seemed to be stuck. The morning stretched on and on. When it's almost recess, it's always hard to pay attention to the teacher, even a wonderful teacher like Mrs. Gunderson.

Lola looked at the clock ten times between 9:33 and 9:34. "Recess is never going to get here!" she thought. "If it's 9:34 and recess starts at 12:20, how many minutes do I have to wait?" She tried to do the math. Was it more than a hundred minutes? It seemed like that! There was no way she could wait that long if the clock kept moving so slowly. She was trying to do the math again when she heard her name called.

"Lola," Mrs. Gunderson said, "perhaps you can tell us the answer."

"A hundred and fifty minutes?"

Laughter came from the children sitting around her.

"Lola," Mrs. Gunderson said in a calm voice. "I guess you didn't hear the question. I asked the class if anyone knew why Elizabeth Cady Stanton was an important person in history?"

ELIZABETH CADY STANTON

"Wasn't she the star of the women's soccer team that won the World Cup in 1999?"

"No, you're thinking of Mia Hamm," Mrs. Gunderson said. "Elizabeth Cady Stanton fought against slavery and to give women the right to vote."

"Wow, I wasn't even close!" Lola made a crooked, uncertain smile. She felt embarrassed.

Mrs. Gunderson nodded sympathetically. Then she put her hands on her hips and looked around the room. "Children, as you know, this is Women's History Month. We're going to split into groups of four. Each group will produce a report on an important event in women's history."

The classroom got quieter than usual.

"You're free to do any kind of report you choose. You may write an essay. You may compose a song. You may build a website. You may make a poster. Surprise me."

The mood in the classroom brightened slightly.

"Can we pick our own groups?" a boy named Bryce asked.

When Mrs. Gunderson said yes, everyone cheered. When she said each group had to be a mix of boys and girls, everyone moaned.

Lola didn't want to choose between Maya and Fayth, so she asked her friend Eva to be in her group. Eva asked Bryce to join, and Bryce asked Howie. The four of them found a quiet corner of the room and sat down to make plans. Eva, Bryce, and Howie did most of the talking. Lola still felt a little embarrassed.

"Hey, I've got an idea," Howie said. "Let's do Elizabeth Cady Stanton!"

"Why?" Eva asked.

"Because we already know Mrs. Gunderson likes her!"

"That's true," Eva said. "But I'd rather pick someone more modern. What about Rosa Parks? Or Michelle Obama?"

"What about the person Lola said? Mia Hamm!" said Bryce. "We could make a video about how her team won the World Cup!"

Lola was no longer counting the minutes until recess. She was not embarrassed anymore, either. "That sounds fun!" she said.

ROSA PARKS

MICHELLE OBAMA

MIA HAMM

6.

Dinner Guests

Gabriel and his grandfather, Francisco, were coming to dinner. That afternoon, Lola stood at the kitchen counter, chopping vegetables. Her mother was preparing her special macaroni and cheese, which she made with elbow noodles, three kinds of cheese, plus salsa, chopped red peppers, and avocado. It tasted even better than it looked.

"Do I have to sit next to Gabriel tonight?" Lola asked. "I'm sure I won't have anything to say to him."

"Are boys really so bad?" Lillian Jones asked.

"Yes, as a matter of fact, they are," Lola said.

"They have no scope for imagination. They're small-minded, overly confident, and *wearisome*. That's a big word for tiring."

"*All* boys?" Ms. Jones snatched a carrot from Lola's cutting board and popped it in her mouth.

"I don't know about *all* of them. But at my school, *a lot* of them are. And Gabriel is part of the problem. Even though he doesn't play soccer, he helps the boys come up with their strategies to keep the girls from getting the ball. It's *so* mean."

"Maybe he's doing it to make friends."

"Do you really think that's OK, Mom?"

"Maybe not," Ms. Jones said. "Maybe you should ask Gabriel why he only helps the boys."

"Isn't it obvious?" Lola asked. "It's because *he's* a boy."

"Mmm-hmm." Lillian Jones turned and gave Lola a hard stare. Lola called it the Interrogation Stare.

Long before Lola understood that her mother was a police officer, she knew about the Interrogation Stare. Lola got the Interrogation Stare every time her mother wanted her to think a little harder about her answer. When she was three years old, she drew on the wall with a permanent marker and told her mother that a unicorn did it. That was the first time she could remember getting the Interrogation Stare. But even as she got older and learned not to lie, Lola continued to get the Interrogation Stare. She hated it.

"*What?* What did I say?" Lola asked. "Why am I getting that stare?"

"You tell me," Lola's mother said.

Lola huffed and went to her room. She stretched out on her bed, looked up at the poster of Team USA, and picked up her library book on soccer strategy.

Lola opened to the first page and began to read: "Have you ever seen the movie *Star Wars*? What if I told you Luke, Leia, and Han had all the advantages in fighting Darth Vader? What if I told you that they knew they could defeat the Galactic Empire because they understood that speed was more important than size in their battle? And what if I told you that winning at soccer is easy when you understand what's important and what isn't?"

Lola kept reading as the house filled with the smell of baked noodles and garlic bread. She was beginning the third chapter of *Smarter Soccer* when she heard the timer on the oven ding, followed minutes later by the buzzer at the front door.

"Lola! Get the door, please!" her mother called.

Lola shuffled down the hall. She opened the door and Gabriel and his grandfather stepped inside.

"Hola, Lola." Gabriel's grandfather smiled and handed Lola a bouquet of yellow tulips. "These flowers are for you and your mother."

"They're from my grandfather," Gabriel said. "Not me."

Francisco Contento gently nudged his grandson as if to say, "Behave yourself."

Lola smiled.

"Thank you for the flowers, Mr. Contento. Hi, Gabriel," she said. "Come in, both of you. May I take your coats?"

At the dinner table, the grown-ups talked about the giant grocery store that opened on Belmont Avenue and about the city's new mayor and about the rising costs of a lot of things that didn't really concern Lola. She felt she should talk to Gabriel, but she didn't know what to say. She certainly couldn't talk about soccer. It would only make her angry again. Finally, she had an idea.

"Hey, Gabriel," she said, between bites of mac and cheese. "Have you ever read *Anne of Green Gables*?"

Gabriel was moving noodles around his plate but not eating. He looked up and shook his head. "What's it about?"

"About 300 pages!" Lola said.

Gabriel's eyebrows scrunched and he scratched his head. "Huh?"

"That was a joke," Lola said. "Anyway, it's about an orphan girl named Anne who goes to live on a farm with two grown-ups who really wanted a boy orphan, not a girl orphan. Anne talks too much and uses a lot of big words, but the grown-ups get used to her. At school there's this boy named Gilbert who teases her. Anne's really smart and competes with that boy to see who's the smartest kid in class."

Gabriel moved more noodles around on his plate. "I bet you the girl turns out to be the smartest," he said.

"Really?" Lola asked. "Why?"

"Because the book is named *Anne of Green Gables*, not *Gilbert of Green Gables*, right? Kind of obvious."

Lola admitted that was a good point, even though she wasn't sure if Anne would turn out to be smarter than Gilbert, or if they would get to be friends or even if it mattered. She hadn't finished the book yet.

Gabriel went back to playing with his food. Mr. Contento was bragging about Gabriel's older brother, who was only a freshman in high school but already playing on the soccer team. He said that Gabriel's father had been the captain of his high school team. Gabriel's mother had played soccer, too, and would have won a scholarship to play in college if she hadn't hurt her knee.

Lola stared at Gabriel as she listened. It looked like the elbow noodles on his plate were arranged in some kind of pattern. He moved one noodle at

a time. Lola thought the pattern looked familiar, but when Gabriel noticed her stare he scrambled the food into a big pile and took a bite. A few noodles bounced from his plate to the floor. Gabriel bent to pick them up. As he sat up again, he hit his head on the table. He rubbed his head and smiled as he sat back up.

"Are you OK?" Lola asked.

Gabriel turned red and said he was fine.

Lola looked at his plate again for a few minutes until she figured out why the noodle patterns there had looked familiar.

"Mom," she said, "may Gabriel and I be excused for a few minutes? I want to show him something in my room."

"Of course, honey," Lillian Jones said. "We'll call you when it's time for dessert."

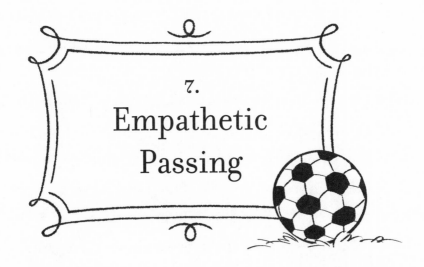

7.
Empathetic Passing

Lola marched into her room, with Gabriel trailing. She opened her desk drawer and pulled out the drawings that Grampa Ed had made after reading the first chapters of *Smarter Soccer*.

"Is this what you were doing with your noodles?" she asked. "Were you making soccer plays?"

When Gabriel blushed and stammered, Lola knew she was right.

"Have you read this book?" she asked, reaching for her copy of *Smarter Soccer*.

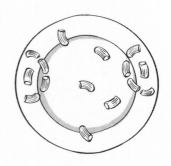

"No." Gabriel picked up the book and looked at the front and back covers. "I get my plays from video games."

Lola's eyes went wide. "How do you do *that*?"

"I play a lot of video games. And I mean *a lot*. But sometimes I don't try to win. I just study the computer's moves. The programmers have analyzed the best soccer teams in the world. So, if I can figure out the moves in the video game, I should learn how to play better soccer."

"And you're using this to coach the boys at recess?"

"Trying." Gabriel frowned. "It doesn't work. The boys never do what they're supposed to."

"I don't understand," said Lola. "Why don't you join the game and make the moves yourself?"

"No, no...I can't. I need to control the whole team to see if my strategy works. And I can't. Even if I did play, the other guys still wouldn't do what I want them to."

"That's because the boys are not *empathetic*," Lola said.

Gabriel laughed. "Is that one of your big words from *Anne of Green Gables*?"

"Actually, it's from *Smarter Soccer*." Lola turned the book over in her hands. "The author says that winning soccer players need to be speedy. That's probably the most important thing...make speedy passes. But good soccer players also need to be *empathetic*, according to the author. That means players need to understand one another. For example, don't just yell, 'Howie! Howie! Pass it to me!' I'm supposed to think about where Howie wants me to be so he can make a good, speedy pass, and then get to that spot. And then if Howie goes to an even better spot, I'm supposed to pass it right back to him. Fast!"

"Empathetic passing," Gabriel said.

"Yes!" Lola said.

"That makes sense," Gabriel said. "But I can't get those guys to pass at all. All they want to do is shoot."

"That's because they're cavemen," Lola said.

Gabriel looked up from the book. "What do you mean?"

"Never mind," Lola said. "But maybe there's a way we can work together. You can test your video-game soccer strategy, and I can figure out how to get the boys to pass the ball to girls."

"How?" Gabriel asked.

"I'm not sure yet." Lola rubbed her chin. "But if you teach me how to play your computer game, maybe I'll think of something."

8.
Goals! Goals! Goals!

That night Lola dreamed she was a soccer player in a video game, and that she was faster and more skilled than all the other video-game soccer players. She scored three goals. She was about to score a fourth when the morning sun slanted through the blinds in her bedroom and woke her.

Meanwhile, Grampa Ed dreamed that his bald head had suddenly grown beautiful brown, curly hair. Lillian Jones dreamed of driving a convertible along curvy mountain roads in California. They were both already awake and in the kitchen when Lola got there. It was Saturday, which meant

SCORE
100 / 0

Lola Lv 50
HP

Howie Lv 1
HP

Grampa made pancakes for Lola and Lola made coffee for Grampa and Lola practiced soccer in the park with her mother. Lola ate quickly and asked if she could go to Gabriel's house.

"You don't want to practice soccer?" her mother asked.

"Maybe later," Lola said. "But I really want to see this video game Gabriel told me about."

"So, you guys are friends now?" Ms. Jones asked.

"Oh, definitely not," Lola said. "But I think he might have scope for imagination. We'll see."

Lola walked through the alley. It was a warm, bright day. Lola breathed in the smell of the damp leaves from last night's rain, and bacon from Stella's Diner on Broadway. "I wish they made candles that smelled like damp leaves and bacon," she thought, as she broke into a run down to Gabriel's building.

Gabriel's apartment was big and full of sunlight. Gabriel's parents, his grandfather, and his brother, Tony, were all in the kitchen. Tony wore a sweatshirt that said "Avondale High School Varsity Soccer" on the front. Gabriel's parents acted surprised to see Lola. She wasn't sure why. Maybe Gabriel didn't get a lot of visitors.

"May I take Lola to the game room?" Gabriel asked. His parents nodded, and he led Lola down the hall.

"My brother and I decided to share a room so we could turn the other bedroom into a game room," Gabriel said as they walked. "It's cool. Wait until you see it."

It *was* cool. The room had a big TV, a computer, a whole shelf full of board games, and another shelf full of books. Two giant beanbag chairs sat in front of the TV. But the coolest thing in the room by far was the set of monkey bars hanging from the ceiling.

"Whoa! You have monkey bars *in your house*?"

"Yup."

"Can I try?"

"My dad's a mechanic. He says it's safe as long as long as you don't weigh more than 300 pounds."

"Well, I *did* eat a lot of pancakes this morning," Lola laughed. "But I think it's OK."

She leaped to grab the first metal bar, swung her legs, and grabbed the second bar. Lola made it from one end of the room to the other on the first try. When she plopped down to the floor her hands were red and achy.

"Nice!" Gabriel said.

"Thanks!" Lola said. "You do it now! I bet you're really good at!"

"Maybe later." Gabriel sat on one of the bean-bag chairs and pulled out two remote controls for his video game. He handed one to Lola, who flopped down on the other beanbag.

"I like car-racing games best, but soccer is cool, too," he said.

Lola and Gabriel played the video soccer game for an hour. The longer they played, the more her grandfather's drawings and the lessons from *Smarter Soccer* made sense.

"You know what's really interesting, Gabriel? The computer only lets me control one player at a time. But look at the players I'm *not* controlling. They hardly move at all. Most of the time they stay in their positions. They don't chase the ball."

"Yeah," Gabriel said. "They play the opposite of the way Howie and Tommy play."

Lola couldn't believe it, but it was true. The two best soccer players at her school were doing everything wrong. They chased the ball all around, tried a lot of fancy moves, and never passed.

"I've been trying to teach them," Gabriel said, "but I'm not doing a good job."

"Maybe we can help them learn to play more like the computer," Lola said.

"How?"

"By trying to understand them. What do the boys really want?"

"They want to score goals," Gabriel said. "That's it. Goals, goals, goals!"

Lola frowned. "They have no scope for imagination."

While Lola and Gabriel talked, some of the players in the video game kept running around. Gabriel controlled the player with the ball and Lola controlled the player defending the ball. But as long as Gabriel didn't pass or shoot and Lola didn't try to make a steal, the soccer ball didn't move. The other players—the ones controlled by the computer—ran around waiting, trying to get open.

"Hey, Gabriel, look at that!" Lola said. "They're running around the field. No one is passing it to

them, but they keep running around anyway and hoping for a pass! Just like the girls at recess!"

"They never give up, do they?" Gabriel said as he watched the little figures on the screen running back and forth without the ball.

"Whoa! That gives me an idea." Lola rubbed her chin. "What if the girls played their own game at recess? What if we used our own ball? An *imaginary* ball! And what if we ran around

63

like those players in the video game and we made imaginary passes and scored a bunch of imaginary goals? And when the boys got tired of it, maybe they would pass the *real* ball to us!"

"Yeah! If you ran really good plays, you'd score a ton of imaginary goals, and the boys would see that there's a smarter way to play!" Gabriel ran his hand through his hair. "It would be a score for imagination!"

Lola jumped up from her beanbag chair. "Yes! Score for imagination! That's *it*!"

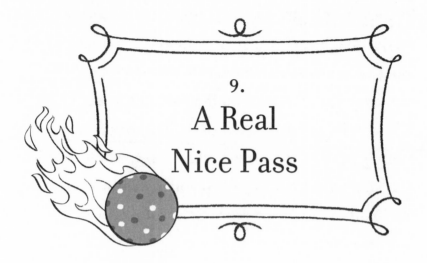

9.

A Real Nice Pass

Lola got to school early on Monday. She zipped her coat to the neck as she stood by the building's entrance, waiting for her friends. The wind blew coldly in her face and the air smelled like rain.

She held some of her grandfather's soccer sketches. Gabriel and Lola had put names on the dots so that the girls who were playing would know exactly where they were supposed to be when the game started.

Lola gave the sketches to Maya, Fayth, and Romy. She also invited a few new girls to join the game. She explained her plan about playing with an imaginary ball. "I think we should ask Charlotte, Zayd, and Edith to play because they're extremely empathetic," Lola had explained to Gabriel when they were assigning positions. "And I want to invite Antoinette, because she just moved here from France and she's been sitting alone under a tree at recess, and we simply have to explore her scope for imagination."

"Are any of them good soccer players?" Gabriel had asked.

"We'll find out!" Lola said.

At recess, Tommy and Howie picked the teams, as usual.

"Better get started," said Mr. Nick. "Looks like rain."

Lola was on Howie's team, along with Romy, Charlotte, Zayd, and three boys. Tommy's team had Fayth, Maya, Edith, Antoinette, and three more boys.

Lola gathered all the girls in a huddle to remind them of her special instructions. "Just remember not to look at their ball," she said. "Remember that we're going to play an imaginary game at the same time as their real game. *Only* look at the *imaginary* ball. Close your eyes and picture it in your mind. It's bright purple with orange polka dots and it has flames shooting out of it. The harder you kick it, the more flames it will shoot. But you have to kick it quick so it doesn't set your shoes on fire. Got it?"

Everyone shouted, "Got it!" and the game began.

At first, the boys thought the girls weren't playing at all. It took them a few minutes to realize the girls were playing their own game with an imaginary ball.

"Um, Lola!" Howie called. "You do realize that you don't have a soccer ball, right?"

"Sorry, Howie? Did you say something? I wasn't paying attention because I just made a perfect pass and Romy just scored her third goal. Nice shot, Romy!"

After ten minutes it began to rain and everyone went inside.

Lola and the girls played with their imaginary purple and orange flaming soccer ball again on Tuesday, Wednesday, and Thursday. While the boys ran all over the field, the girls stayed in their assigned positions. They darted back and forth along short routes. They took imaginary shots only when the imaginary ball arrived near the goal in a perfect imaginary pass.

By Friday, the boys got angry.

"They're ruining everything!" Tommy said, as the boys huddled before the game. "If they don't want to play real soccer, they should go away and let us have the field."

"Gabriel, you're supposed to be our coach!" Howie said. "What should we do?"

Gabriel had been waiting for this moment, but he acted as if he had to think about it. He paused and scratched his head.

"All right, I've got an idea," he finally said. The boys bent into the huddle. "The girls are acting like they don't care about the game. They know they're not as good as we are. They know they can't *really* compete with the boys. That's why they're trying to ruin our game. But I know how we can get rid of them once and for all. Listen up, guys. Next time you see one of the girls wide open and cutting toward the goal, pass her the *real* ball. She won't be able to resist a perfect pass. She'll kick it…and, of course, she'll miss. Then the girls will realize they're wasting their time. They'll give up and we'll have the soccer field forever!"

"Good idea!" Tommy said.

The game began.

"Nice one, Antoinette!" Lola shouted as she received a perfect imaginary pass.

"Hey, Lola, look left!" Maya yelled. Lola looked left and spotted Maya wide open for another imaginary pass.

Maya fired an imaginary shot toward the goal. "Darn it!" she shouted. "It hit the upright and bounced away."

"I'll get it!" Edith sang as she ran to the bushes to retrieve the imaginary ball.

Tommy was so busy paying attention to Maya's imaginary shot that he didn't notice when the real ball came his way. It hit him in the nose.

"Ouch!" Tommy shouted. The shot in the face made his nose numb and his vision bleary. He shook his head, looked down, and tapped the soccer ball—the real soccer ball—with his right foot.

"Hey, Tommy!" Gabriel shouted from the sideline, "Lola is wide open on your right!" Tommy had to think for a second. It had been a long time since he had passed the ball to a girl. Wait! Had he ever passed the ball to a girl?

Tommy booted the ball to Lola, who had found a gap between two defenders and had cut toward the goal. The pass reached Lola with such speed and accuracy that she couldn't help herself. She couldn't bear the thought of wasting such a wonderful chance. And, oh, it felt so good to connect with a real soccer ball again! With one quick swing of her foot she sent the real ball zooming into the real net for a real goal.

Lola didn't stop running. She jogged over to Tommy, putting her hand up for a high-five.

"Nice pass, Tommy," she said.

Tommy smiled.

"I guess you could call it *real* nice," he said.

"I guess you could," Lola said.

10.
So Awesome!

After recess, Mrs. Gunderson turned down the lights in the classroom and turned on the big television at the back of the classroom. It was time for Lola's group to show the class their Women's History Month project.

Bryce's face came on the screen and he began to speak in a very serious voice.

Ladies and gentlemen, welcome to one of the biggest sporting events of all time, the 1999 World Cup. In 1999, cell phones and women's soccer were not popular at all. Can you believe it? My name is Bryce. And before the big game starts, I'm going to interview one of the best soccer players in the world. Her name is Mia Hamm.

Lola appeared in a T-shirt that said MIA HAMM across the front. She had a soccer ball under her arm.

Hi, Bryce, I'm Mia Hamm. I was born in 1972 in Selma, Alabama, and I'm an awesome soccer player.

Yes, you are! Mia, can you tell us how you got so awesome?

Well, Bryce, there's a rule called Title Nine that says colleges have to let women plays sports just like men. Thanks to that rule, I got a scholarship to play soccer in college. And once I had that scholarship I worked very hard to do my best. As Anne says in Anne of Green Gables, *it's delightful to have ambitions, and I have a lot! That's how I got to be so awesome!*

Everyone in the classroom clapped. The camera turned back to Bryce.

Now I'm going to interview Mia's coach. Coach, can you tell us what makes Mia Hamm so awesome?

Eva came on the TV, dressed in a T-shirt that said COACH.

Of course I can tell you, Bryce. It's because she understands that good teams share. They don't leave anyone out. Mia is the star of our team, but she always passes the ball. She makes sure everyone gets a turn to play. That makes the whole team stronger. And now, if you'll excuse me, the game is about to start! And we're going to give it our all—together!"

The lights came on in the classroom and everyone cheered. Mrs. Gunderson smiled and told the group they'd earned an A-plus.

11.
Good and Tired

The third-grade boys and girls learned many things that chilly day in March. They learned that Antoinette was an excellent soccer player. They learned that it was much easier to score goals when they were spaced out on the field and made quick passes and didn't chase the ball too much. In Mrs. Gunderson's class, they learned that Elizabeth Cady Stanton was the first woman to run for Congress.

But they didn't learn how Gabriel and Lola had worked together to hatch the plan that solved their soccer problems.

"Do you think they'll ever figure it out?" Gabriel asked Lola as they walked home from school together.

"We'll see," Lola said. "I have to admit that some of the boys have shown more scope for imagination than I had expected."

"Have you finished that book yet?" Gabriel asked. "What was it called again? *Gilbert of Green Gables*?"

"Ha-ha! Very funny! I'm almost done. It turns out that Gilbert wasn't really mean. Anne was just being *obstinate*. That means stubborn."

Gabriel nodded. "And who turned out to be the smartest student in their school, Anne or Gilbert?"

"Oh, I'm not telling," Lola said. "You'll have to read the book."

"Maybe I will."

"Maybe you won't."

"Yeah, you're right. Maybe I won't."

Gabriel laughed.

"You know what, Gabriel?" Lola asked. "You're funny."

"Thanks."

"I'm glad we're friends now," she said.

"Me, too."

"But there's still one thing about you I don't get."

Gabriel turned to her. "What?"

Lola stopped walking and looked at Gabriel. "Why don't you play soccer with us? And why didn't you swing on your monkey bars?"

Lola waited. But Gabriel didn't answer.

Lola waited longer.

Gabriel still didn't answer.

"You don't have to tell me," she said finally.

"OK," Gabriel said. "I'll tell you. But you'll probably think I'm a wimp."

"Maybe I will!"

Gabriel laughed. "It's pretty simple really...I stink. And not just at soccer. I'm bad at all sports. I'm super clumsy. I even drool toothpaste on my shirt practically every time I brush my teeth." Gabriel looked down at his shirt and pointed to a small stain. "See!"

82

Lola cracked up. "I'm glad it's nothing serious," she said.

"Well, it is *kind of* serious," Gabriel said. "My brother got all the talent and I got none."

"Sorry," Lola said. "I didn't mean to laugh. I'm kind of bad at soccer, too. But, you know what, I'll bet your brother isn't as smart or funny as you are."

"Actually, he's incredibly smart. And super funny."

"Well then he's too perfect. Nobody likes people who are too perfect."

"But *I* like him!"

"Wow, Gabriel," Lola said. "I'm trying to be supportive, but you're not making it easy."

"It's no big deal," Gabriel said. "I'm not sad or mad about it. I like being different. And I love watching soccer and coaching. I really don't need to play. But, hey, thanks for being an *empathetic* listener."

ele

That night, Lola made mac and cheese without any help from her mother or grandfather. Instead of salsa, peppers, and avocado, she mixed in tomatoes, black olives, and spinach. Grampa Ed made the salad.

"I had coffee with your teacher this afternoon," Grampa Ed said. Grampa Ed and Mrs. Gunderson were friends. "She asked me what book you were going to read after *Anne of Green Gables*."

"I haven't decided yet," Lola said. "What was *your* favorite book when you were my age, Grampa?"

Grampa Ed scratched his head. "To be honest, I didn't read that much when I was a kid."

"Oh, that means you're lucky, Grampa, because you have more books to explore now. Reading a new book is like making a new friend. When you finish a book you love, it's like saying goodbye to your friend. But it's not sad because you can see her again whenever you want! Oh, that gives me an idea, Grampa! Would you like to borrow my copy of *Anne of Green Gables*?"

"What's it about?" Grampa Ed asked. "And don't say it's *about 300 pages!*"

Lola laughed. So did Grampa Ed. As they set the table for dinner, Lola told Grampa Ed all about the book. Lola's mother walked in the front door just as the burbling pan of mac and cheese came out of the oven.

"Wow, it smells *so* good in here!" Lillian Jones said as she took off her jacket and hung it in the closet.

Lola ran down the hall and hugged her.

Her mother hugged her back. "How was school today, sweetie?"

"Don't ask about school," Grampa Ed said. "Ask about recess. That's where all the exciting stuff happens."

"Grampa's right," Lola said. "Recess *has* been exciting lately. And today was especially exciting. Today was *transcendent*. That means above the normal possibilities."

"That's a strong word," Lillian Jones said. "So, what made it *transcendent*?"

"Our plan finally worked! The boys got tired of watching us play imaginary soccer and they started passing the ball to us. And I scored a goal!"

"That's amazing, Lola!"

"Well," said Grampa Ed, "if boys can pass the ball to girls, I guess that proves cavemen don't have to be cavemen all their lives."

"That reminds me of a riddle, Grampa," Lola said. "Why was school easier for cavemen and cavewomen?"

Grampa Ed bit his lower lip. "I give up. Why?"

"Because they didn't have to study history!"

Grampa Ed gave a little laugh. So did Lola's mom.

After dinner, Lola and her mother cleared the table. Grampa Ed sat on the couch and read the newspaper.

"Soccer in the park tomorrow morning?" Lola's mother asked.

"Definitely," Lola said. "I'll need to get used to kicking a real ball again."

Lola hugged her mother and grandfather and said goodnight to both of them. After putting on her pajamas and brushing her teeth, she climbed into bed and opened *Smarter Soccer* to Chapter Nine, which was called "Scoring Goals."

"*Ironically*," the author wrote, "you'll score more goals if you kick a little softer and keep the ball low. It takes twice as long for a goalie to bend down low than to reach up high." Lola grabbed the pencil and notepad on her nightstand and jotted down the word *ironically* so she could look up its definition in the morning.

As she got under the covers and prepared for sleep, she closed her eyes and pictured a soccer game. In her mind she could see her friends—the boys and the girls—playing on a TV screen. They were big and strong and extremely talented. They had beautiful uniforms and played on real grass in a real stadium. All their passes were sharp, fast, and *empathetic*.

Lola thought about how lucky she was to have found the right words and the right books and the right friends to solve her problem, and how good it felt to go to sleep when your muscles—especially your legs—were tired from an exciting game of soccer and how much fun it would be to start the next day with rested legs and a new burst of morning sun and chocolate-chip pancakes for breakfast.